POKÉMON

Bagon Can Fly!

**Adapted by Tracey West
and Katherine Noll**

OFFICIAL
Pokémon
MASTER'S
CLUB

SCHOLASTIC INC.

New York   Toronto   London   Auckland   Sydney
Mexico City   New Delhi   Hong Kong   Buenos Aires

Published by Scholastic Inc.
90 Old Sherman Turnpike, Danbury, CT 06816.

SCHOLASTIC and associated logos are trademarks and/or registered trademarks of
Scholastic Inc.

ISBN 0-439-72184-9

First Scholastic Printing, March 2005

**Ash and his friends were
walking through the mountains.
Some rocks fell down from
a high cliff. They all looked up.**

A small blue Pokémon stood on the cliff.

"Whoa!" Ash said. "What is *that?*"

Ash's Pokédex had the answer. "Bagon, the Rock Head Pokémon," said the little computer. "Bagon is a Dragon Type."

"Bagon has a very strong Skull Bash attack," Max said.

May was nervous. "I hope it does not attack us."

Just then Bagon jumped off of the cliff!

Ash and the others ran out of the way.

Crash! Bagon landed in the dirt. But it did not get hurt, thanks to its hard head.

"I think Bagon is looking for a fight," said Max.

"Fine then," Ash said. "Taillow, I choose you!"

Taillow flew out of its Poké Ball. It zoomed at Bagon. Bagon climbed back up the mountain.

Bagon jumped off of the cliff
again! It landed with another crash.
Then a girl ran up to Bagon.
She wore strange glasses.

"Stop attacking my Bagon!"
she yelled.

"Bagon attacked us first!" Ash said.
"Bagon swooped down on us from
the cliff!" May added.

The girl did not look mad anymore.
"Sorry," she said. "I did not know
what happened."

"No problem," said Brock. "My name is Brock. Who are you?"

"Michelle," the girl answered.

"Michelle," Brock sighed. "What a beautiful name!"

Bagon climbed back up the cliff. Then it jumped off again!

Michelle looked through her glasses. "Change direction 80 degrees!" she ordered.

Bagon landed on the ground. Then it bounced into Michelle's arms.

"What do those glasses do?" Max asked.

"They have a computer inside them," Michelle explained. "They help Bagon make better moves in battle."

"But why does Bagon keep jumping off the cliff?" Brock asked.

"Bagon wants to learn to fly," Michelle said.

"But Bagon evolves into Shelgon," Brock said. "And Shelgon evolves into Salamence. Only Salamence can fly, right?"

"Right," Michelle said. "But Bagon cannot wait. I am giving it extra help so it can evolve faster."

Nearby, Team Rocket was hiding. "I think the Boss might like that Bagon," Meowth said. "Its hard head could come in handy!"

Ash did not know Team Rocket was after Bagon.

"My Pikachu will battle your Bagon," Ash told Michelle. "The battle will make Bagon stronger."

"This should be good," Max said. "Pikachu is an Electric Type. They are usually not good against Dragon Types."

Ash made the first move.
"Quick Attack, Pikachu!" he yelled.
Pikachu raced toward Bagon.

Michelle used her special glasses.

"Bagon, move 30 degrees to the left," she said.

Bagon moved and lowered its head. *Bam!* It slammed Pikachu with a Skull Bash.

"Pikachu, use Thunderbolt!"
Ash yelled.

Pikachu hurled an electric blast
at Bagon. May used her glasses.
She told Bagon how to dodge it.

Then Bagon hit Pikachu with
Skull Bash. Pikachu was really hurt
this time!

"Hang in there, Pikachu!" Ash said. "Let's show them what we've got!"

"*Pika!*" Pikachu said. It got back on its feet.

Pikachu smacked Bagon with Iron Tail!

Slam! Bagon went flying.

The little Dragon Pokémon slowly got back on its feet. But a loud noise stopped the battle.

Everyone looked up. A helicopter was flying above them!

"It is Team Rocket!" cried Ash.

Meowth flew out of the helicopter using a jet pack. Jessie moved the jet pack with a remote control.

Meowth swooped down and grabbed Bagon!

"Treecko, I choose you!" Ash yelled.

Ash's Grass Pokémon popped out of its Poké Ball.

Treecko hit the helicopter with Bullet Seed.

The remote control fell out of Jessie's hands. She could not control the jet pack. Meowth and Bagon went zooming over the trees.

Jessie and James followed them in the helicopter.

Michelle grabbed the remote control. Then she and the others ran after them.

Slam! Meowth and Bagon crashed into a tree. Jessie and James got to them first.

Bagon took the jet pack. *"Bagon! Bagon!"* it said.

"Bagon says it wants to use the jet pack to fly," Meowth said.

"That is just silly," Jessie said.

"I bet the Boss would really like a *flying* Bagon," Meowth added.

Then Ash and his friends arrived.

"Think again," Ash said. "Pikachu, use Quick Attack!"

Pikachu slammed Team Rocket into the helicopter.

But Team Rocket was not down
yet. They quickly grabbed Pikachu.
Then they flew off.

Bagon strapped on the jet pack. Treecko jumped on its back. Then the two Pokémon took off after the helicopter.

Bagon slammed into the helicopter with its hard head. Treecko blasted open Pikachu's cage with Bullet Seed. Then Pikachu jumped out of the helicopter. It landed on Bagon's back with Treecko. The three Pokémon flew away.

But they had one more thing to do. *"Pikachuuuuuu!"* Pikachu zapped Team Rocket with a Thunderbolt.

"It looks like we are blasting off again!" Team Rocket cried.

Bagon zipped and zoomed across the sky.

"Hey, check out Bagon flying around!" May said.

Max smiled. "Michelle believed in the little Pokémon, and its dream came true."

Bagon landed. Michelle hugged it.

"How did you like your first flight?" she asked.

"*Bagon!*" the Pokémon cried. Then it began to glow . . .

Bagon evolved into Shelgon!

"You did it, Shelgon," Michelle said. "You never gave up."

"It is good to hold on to your dreams," Ash said. "Right, Pikachu?"

Pikachu smiled. *"Pika! Pika!"*

Who's That Dragon Pokémon?

37

See page 45 or your
Dragon & Poison Pokédex
for the answer.

Mouthing Off!

Can you tell who these Poison Pokémon are by just looking at each one's mouth?

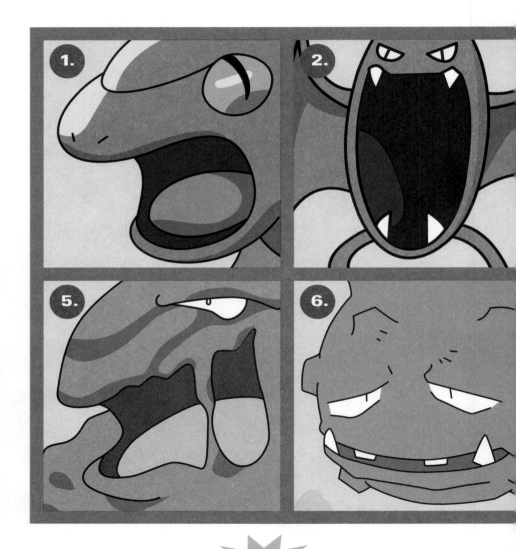

3.

4.

7.

8.

39

Check page 45 or your
Dragon & Poison Pokédex
for the answers.

Battle Time!

Now it is your turn to battle! Read about each battle below. Then pick the best Pokémon to use against your opponent. In each battle, all of the Pokémon are the same level.

1. "Bagon, go!" your opponent shouts. Which Pokémon will you choose to face this little Dragon Pokémon?

Mawile™
(Steel)

Charmander™
(Fire)

Treecko™
(Grass)

2. Yuck! You are facing Muk, a smelly Poison Type. Which of these Pokémon has the best chance to beat it?

Shroomish™
(Grass)

Rattata™
(Normal)

Dusclops™
(Ghost)

3. Your opponent chooses Arcanine. Which of these Pokémon will do best against this Fire Type?

Staryu™
(Water)

Nidorina™
(Poison)

Altaria™
(Dragon/Flying)

Check page 45 or your *Pokédex* books for the answers.

One Day I'll Fly!

None of the Pokémon on these pages can fly. But one in each row will evolve into a Flying Type. Can you pick out the Pokémon in each row that will evolve into a Flying Pokémon?

1. Numel™   Shelgon™   Kecleon™

2. Magikarp™   Goldeen™   Mudkip™

3. Torchic™   Charmeleon™   Slugma™

4. Larvitar™ Eevee™ Dragonair™

5. Togepi™ Igglybuff™ Teddiursa™

6. Spinarak™ Surskit™ Paras™

7. Pineco™ Sunkern™ Silcoon™

43

Check page 45 or your *Ultimate Sticker Book* for the answers.

Dragon & Poison Pokémon Jokes

What do you get
if you cross
a Seviper and
a hot dog?

A fangfurter!

Why was Ash
able to catch the
Dragonite?

*Because it was
draggin' its feet!*

What happened to
the Golbat when it
lost a battle?

It went batty!

What is Ekans's
favorite subject?

Hiss-tory

What is the
best thing about
a bunch of Koffing?

*They have
poisonality!*

What time is it
when Salamence sits
on a fence?

*Time to get
a new fence!*